If I Could Do Life Again

By Chris Love

Tate Publishing, LLC

If I Could do Life Again by Chris Love
Copyright © 2005 by Chris Love. All rights reserved.

Published in the United States of America
by Tate Publishing, LLC
127 East Trade Center Terrace
Mustang, OK 73064
(888) 361–9473

Book design copyright © 2005 by Tate Publishing, LLC. All rights reserved.

No part of this publication may be reproduced, stored in a retrieval system or transmitted in any way by any means, electronic, mechanical, photocopy, recording or otherwise without the prior permission of the author except as provided by USA copyright law.

This novel is a work of fiction. Names, descriptions, entities and incidents included in the story are products of the author's imagination. Any resemblance to actual persons, events and entities is entirely coincidental.

ISBN: 1–9331487–3-X

Dedication

This book is dedicated to the two women in my life, my wife Karen and my mom Mary. I can always depend on them for love, support, and brutally honest feedback.

Chapter 1

At first glance, Thomas Sullivan could give the idle observer cause to do a double take. There was something there, in the eyes especially. His features no doubt revealed years of abuse. Used to be Tom would have nothing but the best, Grey Goose, soda with a lime. In certain circles it was half-believed that this premium vodka, after an evening of indulgence, would somehow rob you of the "Blue Meanies." At least that's what Tom and his buddies would tell each other.

The "Blue Meanies," other than being a saying introduced by the Beatles in their more experimental years, was a humorous way of describing a hangover. The wives obviously knew too well, much better, that the hangover was not robbed, maybe hidden.

Cigarettes were a kind of game for Tom. He could smoke a pack in an evening and then go two months without a one. Though as time progressed, those months turned into weeks, days, and then minutes between smokes. Actually, he had cut back to a pack and a half a day. His lungs didn't seem to lock up if he kept at that level of intake. His legs were weak and had bad circulation, so it seemed ironic that he had the ½ mile track record as a sophomore.

Tammy used to actually be jealous about how the other "stay-at-home moms" admired Tom so. He seemed to have some kind of genetic ability to stay looking and acting young before it all fell apart. It's amazing how when things go wrong all the God-given talent tends to fall by the wayside.

Well, today, Mr. Sullivan was having some serious difficulties. It is really a sad thing to see a man who causes so much of his own deterioration. His vital organs operated at half-mast. His once-nerves-of-steel seemed to short circuit on occasion. Moods ran in all different directions without any advance notice. Thirty-two years ago, friends would praise Tommy for his youthful appearance and spirit. Self-loathing can take away any appearances. If given the right circumstances, this state of mind can either drive a man crazy or slowly eat at his soul. He has learned to be really good at the self-loathing routine, but today was special.

"Sullivan!" yelled the guard. On time for once, Tom thought, as the letter flew through the cell door slot. A personal letter was something to cherish. Animosity would rise among the forgotten prisoners. Tom did not give a damn how anyone in this place felt. He was going to enjoy this correspondence from his ex-wife and go through his normal ritual, reading it complemented with a cup of freeze-dried prison coffee.

Tammy had mellowed over the years and truly felt pity and shame for Tom. So, almost every three months she would update him on the latest. She was really the only one who had kept in contact with him. Thirty-two years is too long to be away from your kids. They were adults now. The girls were married with children of their own. Scotty, the oldest, was only four years away from the age when they put Tom away. Scotty was a successful businessman now.

Tom was on the road to success prior to the incident. Everyone loved and admired him, especially when it was time to celebrate a new account, which seemed to happen a lot prior to his incarceration. Throughout the years, he had thought over and over how the kids were not getting his attention. He wished he could have given them his best. He did not know what his best was.

If he could do it again, he would show everyone what he was really made of. He would be a maniac in this respect. "Could you imagine what kind of courage I could muster up, armed with the knowledge of everything I have been through," he would say to himself. But Tom could not let himself fantasize too much. In the place he was, a daydream could all of a sudden slip into a deep depression. He knew all hope was gone. Depression is a tough enemy to battle, but a letter would help today.

Chapter 2

Tom, this will be my last letter to you. Tom's chest tightened as he quickly jumped out of his cheap plastic prison-issue chair. *What the heck is going on?* he thought. A familiar pain overwhelmed him. Panic set in as he had to stop and assess what this could mean. "Sit down, Sullivan," guards yelled, "or go back to the block!" A couple of eyes looked up from their yellow and white hot stuff (prison-issue eggs and grits). Grits were only served in fifteen prisons across the U.S.; North Carolina was not about to stop serving grits.

Tom was not a big man, but given the right moment, he could shoot lasers with his eyes. His old man taught him that trait. Needless to say, other prisoners respected the crazy stare and passed on eye contact. On top of that, rumor on "C" block was that Tom had been packing a "shank," otherwise known as a homemade knife. Also he was not afraid of death. This combination earned him serious respect. Tom grabbed the letter and left the slop house. He needed privacy. His cell was the place to be for this.

Back in the cell, he calmed himself down. She's just mad at something and taking it out on him as she had done so many times before. She has a right to get this way. Whatever it is he will work it out. If he lost contact with Tammy, he would lose his mind for sure. It wasn't even hope that he had with her. He had just turned 74. There was no hope of getting her back. Doctors say he will probably be dead in a couple of years. Two years on "C" block is like six on the outside.

Having Tammy forgive him helped keep the demons from overrunning his feeble life, and they were surely lurking and watching his every move. Tom still prayed on occasion when he felt it all coming apart. He would often ask himself "why."

What really bothered him was how he was wasting his life prior to the accident. He came to the realization that he was a true fool. He had a beautiful, intelligent and caring wife. She loved him. She gave him three of the most precious children one could ever imagine. He did not appreciate what God had given him.

In his 40's he was very good at keeping himself busy with friends, work, and neighborhood parties. He constantly thought of himself and his own issues. His priorities one and two were: work and himself. Saturday and Sunday mornings were usually difficult, as he tried to give attention to his family. The body would not allow you to forget the night before, Grey Goose or not. Back then, Tom would go through the motions and try to spend time with the family after a night of indulgence, but he knew he could have offered so much more. It must have been confusing for his family because there were times when he would stop drinking as well. This would usually occur when things were going well at work, and he would make a true effort to clean himself up. During these rare times, Tom would come alive. All of a sudden, comedy and laughter were part of the commotion in the Sullivan household.

The kids loved their father so much. They cherished it when Dad wanted to fool around. The little things, like a messy room, would not bother him as it normally would have. Instead, he would take the clothes that were on a bedroom floor, put them on his head, and chase the kids around teasing them.

Tom was a hero to Scotty. He wanted to be with his father any chance he could get. Scotty would always try to impress his dad with whatever sport or academic challenge he had. Susan adored her father. She was a true Daddy's girl. Tom would actually hold back a little, when it came to disciplining her, because he knew it would crush her. Rachel was the baby and unfortunately, did not see the best years of her father.

During his thirty-two years in prison, Tom thought over and over about how much of a fool he had been. He knew it was too late. He loved to hear from Tammy on occasion but was ashamed to try to force a relationship with his children and therefore, resorted to loving them from afar.

As Tom would occasionally allow his mind to wonder about how things could have been, he would inevitably come back to what brought him to this place. What had always driven him "nuts" was the fact that he made a stupid and unforgivable mistake. More, it was the question of what made him act in this manner. Why did he break the law with no regard whatsoever when he had no history or pattern of this in his pre-prison life.

During the trial his friends had attested that Tom was very upset at the party but not as belligerent as the prosecution had portrayed him to be. Belligerency was the prosecution's motive. Although he had a history of drinking, sometimes in an excessive manner, he was always careful to obey the law. Why did he allow himself to act erratically and against his beliefs to commit such a horrible act? Forget about if he, in fact, deserved the consequences. Tom just could not remember. The accident had put him into some sort of shock and disabled him in this manner. Repeating the phrase, "I do not recollect," only affords presidents and people in high places a "get-out-of-jail-free" card. The question of what happened had plagued Tom for decades.

Tom pulled the letter out of his pocket, sat down, and opened it up.

Tom,

This will be my last letter to you. Scotty has had an accident. Just like you, he was drunk and driving.

Although he didn't kill any children like you, he killed himself. He is dead, Tom. He is dead. I hate you. I can't help blaming you for this. You really screwed up our lives. You were his role model as a child, and then you left and caused us so much pain. Scotty was just like you as a young man. I have been trying through the years to put a positive spin on the kids' lives and mine. I am not protecting you any longer. The kids and I will always be deeply scarred because of your actions. I will never feel truly happy again. I will not take any blame for what you did. You treated me badly, even before the accident. I can't give Rick the love he deserves. I am reminded too much of your problems and cannot cope with it anymore. Don't bother writing me. I won't open it. Rick and I have been talking about moving, and I will not forward our address. I hope God forgives you, because I won't.

Tammy

Tom froze with terrifying disbelief. He did not even think he had enough emotion to generate the immense pain that he felt right then. The demons were surely aroused and moving in. "Oh God!" screamed Tom. "Son of a bitch!" he screamed at the top of his lungs.

"Tom, are you alright?" a neighbor yelled over from a cell away.

He hardly heard his friend. His heart was pounding dangerously hard. He ran to his small metal mirror to glare at himself.

It was all hitting him as if he never thought about it before. His face was beet red as he was slipping fast and knew it was going to be all over.

"S—co—tt—y!" He continued to yell his son's name.

Tom did, however, remember Scotty when they dragged his father off to face a life sentence in prison. His boy, who thought of his father as a hero, was stunned. Tom could never forget the look on his son's face.

He was feeling hot, but his fingers were cold.

"Son of a, Son of a . . . God please!" He was slipping fast.

"Sully what's going on? Keep your cool man." A prison mate two cells down tried to calm him.

He had never felt so much anger and self-hate in his life. Primal instincts were taking over. He felt an incredible urge to kill.

Prisoners were starting to rumble as his screams brought attention to the guards. Now, he could only think of one thing and knew time was short. He could not hold it together.

"Dear God, all I wanted to be was . . . I didn't get the chance. . . ." Tom's hands began to shake violently. "Scotty, Scotty!" Tom yelled again, "Oh God," Tom fell to his knees. Time was short. The electric locks unbolted with that familiar loud knock. He knew it was just a matter of minutes before they dragged him out of his cell.

Tom quickly jumped up, reached in his mattress, and pulled out the shank. With a swift motion of his arm, he cocked it back and exposed the right side of his neck. It was going to be over in an instant and nothing could stop it. All he had to do was hit the jugular. By the time the guards arrived, they would have to turn around and grab protective gloves to avoid exposure to a prisoner's blood.

"What's going on Sully? Hold it together."

Larry, another neighbor in the cell across the way tried once more. Tom did not even hear his friend or respond.

Before he released his throw, he realized the demons had won and yelled "I'm sorry!" With that, he threw his right arm with all his strength. The speed was a robotic throw. It had been years since he had such strength and speed.

Chapter 3

The light was extremely bright. In fact, Tom could hardly see. His depth perception was also distorted. Tom felt as though he had just awakened from a long restful sleep, but he wasn't in a bed. He was kneeling on the floor in a large bright room. As he awoke, he realized his most recent actions. The pain was gone. Not just the neck, but the internal emotional pain. "I must be in the hospital," he said in a whisper. "How did I survive?" Tom asked himself.

He reached up slowly to find his neck unscarred and fine. Actually, he noticed it felt different in a good way. It felt muscular and tight as it had years ago. His eyes could not adjust to the light. There was someone walking toward him. "Thomas Timothy John Sullivan," a voice spoke in front of him. The last time someone had called him with all those names was at his Catholic confirmation as a young boy. The manner and tone was one of care and concern, a trait at which the prison did not exactly excel. The voice was also somewhat familiar.

"I'm lost," Tom spoke out.

"We found you, Thomas," the man's voice said, this time a lot closer. A large hand reached down to aide in getting him to his feet. Everything seemed slow and calm.

"Thanks."

"You're more than welcome, Thomas."

"I'm dreaming."

"Yes, it is like a dream, but it is also very real."

"I didn't feel a thing."

"You're not dead, Thomas."

He began to think clearer now. "All right, who are you, and what is this place?"

"My name is Oliver; just call me Ollie. Think of this as a temporary holding place. A place where we can talk, as the Father felt it was a time to stop all this and get involved."

"I have known you for a long time, Thomas. We need to talk about the guilt and pain you are carrying with you. We can't let you move on if you don't reckon with it."

"I murdered a 5-year-old boy, and my son has died," Tom cried out with pain and disgust. Sobbing, Tom continued. "I ruined my life and my family. I don't care what happens to me. I deserve it."

"You are forgiven," Ollie replied. "Little

Ronnie Becker forgives you; he knows it was an unfortunate accident. But you must forgive yourself. I cannot help you if you don't. Lucifer wants you to continue to feel this way. We are not giving up this fight yet, but we need you to help us. I know you have a good soul, Thomas, and we don't want to lose a good soul."

Tom looked up into Ollie's eyes. He looked so familiar. "Do I know you and how do you know all these things about me?"

"I have been with you all your life," Ollie replied. "You are only thinking about a terrible tragedy in your life. I've seen you do some remarkable, generous deeds. There was a time in your life when we were extremely happy with your growth. You communicated frequently and always had the best intentions for your fellow man."

"You're confused. You don't know what you're talking about," Tom lashed out. "How do you know me? Am I on drugs or something?"

Tom reached for his left front pocket and it was empty. He also found that his chest that he once knew was back—his old friend. It must be a primal thing, but there was nothing like hitting your fist against your own strong chest. Tom began to humble himself, realizing that the person he was addressing had some answers he needed. "Sir, please just tell me what is going on here." Tom would usually have the word "hell" in his last sentence, but something told him to bite his tongue.

"Do me a favor, Thomas and listen."

Tom wondered what was going on. *What was this person's agenda? Why am I . . . ?*

"Care for a little journey, Thomas?"

I don't think I have a choice, he thought to himself.

"You always have a choice and are accountable for all choices. The question is do we make the right choices in life?"

Tom decided not to come back with his normal sarcastic reply. Instead he reached over again at his left pocket and felt his muscular chest again.

"They are not there" Ollie said.

"Huh?" Tom responded, taken off guard.

"Your cigarettes. We don't encourage that sort of thing, so I decided to leave them behind."

At that, Tom looked down at his hands. These were not his hands as he remembered them. The large sores and dark brown patches were gone. The fingernails were no longer tobacco stained.

"Now please do me a favor, walk forward and open that door to the right of you."

"Where?"

"Don't worry, I'm going with you. This path

will take you to the times that I speak of, times before when your choices in life were better."

Tom stared hard and began to approach the foggy opening that Ollie referred to. The light was still very strong but comforting in a way. His legs carried him swiftly toward the unknown passage. He felt that old strength he had long ago. As Tom went to push the door open, he could hear laughter on the other side. The second that he touched the door, he was instantly set upon a beach in front of a young family.

"Tommy!" one of the boys yelled. Tom turned sharply and could not believe his eyes. There in front of him was his little brother Jack, at around 7 years old. Looking around, he noticed a few more faces. Across the beach, he saw himself at age 9 or so. His hair was long and bleached out by the summer sun, and he was running and laughing like he never remembered. He saw Sara and Rachel, his two younger sisters, and Donovan his baby brother.

Mom and Dad were serving lunch. "Oh man, this is that beach town we used to visit for our summer vacations." It must be in the late 1960s, a far cry from 2034. "What is going on, Ollie?" Tom felt choked up as he watched his beautiful Mom serving everyone pizza on the beach. She looked so happy and proud with all the children around her.

"Tommy, get that seashell out of Donovan's mouth," his father spit out laughing.

"I never remember my Dad enjoying himself so much," Tom spoke out in a whisper.

"It's too bad we seem to let the bad times wipe out the good ones," Ollie replied.

As the family finished up their afternoon pizza, young Tom went to retrieve a Frisbee which had been thrown up and over one of the secluded sand dunes. He climbed the hot sand, avoiding the sharp, natural straw grass piercing through the surface of the dune. He caught sight of his blue Frisbee that was halfway buried and ran down the back side of the dune to retrieve it. Tom stopped in his tracks, noticing he was not alone. Lying down in a shaded spot underneath an old abandoned wooden boat was an old man sleeping.

Tom's first thoughts were to run and tell his parents. His curiosity kept him from moving as he decided to observe a little more. He remembered the teachings at Sunday Mass to "love thy brother," even the fallen ones. The man was wearing rags and had long grey unmanaged hair. Tom's heart had begun to sink as he wondered what had brought this person to the place he was—hiding, and sleeping on a beautiful day at the beach, under an old dirty boat. Tom could not see the old man's face but noticed his big, dirty, shoeless feet sticking out of the homemade shelter.

He stepped closer and continued to wonder what the man's predicament was. His heart jumped as the old man stirred a little. Tom wondered how he could help and then slowly reached into his bathing suit pocket, pulling out his week's spending money for boardwalk activities. His emotions gave him a feeling of strength as he moved closer to approach the forgotten man. "Sir, you need this more than me," he said, as he tucked the two tens into the large clenched hands.

Tom jumped again, as the man finally spoke without turning to look up, "God bless you son."

With that, Tom ran quickly, grabbed the Frisbee, and climbed over the backside of the dune. He glanced back, before losing sight of his new forgotten friend.

Ollie looked over at Tom, who seemed to have an expression of surprise on his face.

"We were so proud of you then, Thomas." Tom looked back at him with sad eyes. Ollie went on, "As I remember, you had not told your parents what you had done. You went the whole week without any money and told your family you had lost it. You filled Mr. Raymond Cook's heart with so much love that day. Because of your actions, he went on to do some generous deeds of his own, one of which was to make sure we intervened in your case Thomas."

Young Thomas made it back to where his family was sitting on the beach.

"Did you get the Frisbee, son? It sure took you awhile."

"Yeah, Dad, everything is fine."

"All right, it's time for a race," his father said as he stood up.

"No, please, Tim, the kids just ate," said Mom.

"Come on, who is with me?" Dad continued.

"I'm definitely there," Sara shouted out.

"What kind of a lead are you going to give us, Dad?" Tommy asked, pointing his arm and finger at his father.

"Don't you worry, buddy boy, I'll give you at least 5 or 6 feet."

"Daaaad," everyone chimed in.

"No, I'm just kidding. You guys tell me where to stand."

All at once, in a manner of seconds, just as they arrived, it all lifted away like a cloud. Tom was almost in shock. His mouth was wide open as it all lifted away. All of his senses where alert and functioning properly. He felt a little sad but did not feel as if this emotion would cause him to slip into depression as it usually did. "Man," Tom whispered and then paused, "I loved my family so much at that time. Everything seemed to make sense. We were all supposed to stay together. We were all supposed to stay happy and be successful."

"Thomas, I brought you here to this time because your heart and soul was gold in those days. You looked out for your family and gave all you had to keep things right." Tom started to feel the old pain again. His eyes swelled up.

"It tore my mom apart when they put me away. Dad just climbed deeper into the bottle. My brothers and sisters disowned me."

All of a sudden Tom stared at Ollie in a skeptical manner. "What's going on here? Am I hallucinating? I must be in the prison hospital and on some powerful drugs." Ollie looked at him with a confident sort of smirk.

"Do you really think you would have made it with what you were trying to do? Do you think those guards would have raced you down to the infirmary without a care for themselves?" Ollie was right. There was no way he would have made it. Those guards would have taken their time with the procedures. They would never have risked any type of contamination. There had been 41 suicides or "accidents" since

Tom's incarceration, and probably half of them could have been saved.

"And what is this talk of your friends and family disowning you? As I remember it, you would not let anyone visit you. You tore up letters and told everyone to leave you alone." He began to realize that Ollie had a first-hand account of what had taken place in his life. Although over the years, he had actually made himself believe a lot of fabricated convenient stories.

"Whatever," Tom replied.

"We are far from done. Follow me."

"Follow you where?"

"You are right in front of a passage; I need you to just step on through."

Tom paused, uncertain of what to expect next. He approached a door and heard a lot of voices as he again touched the smoky wall. This time adults were present.

"Tommy boy, get over here and give me a hug," laughed an older woman. It was Grammy O'Connor. Tom realized it was another family gathering. "I must be eight or nine years old again," he observed. They were at Grammy and Pop O'Connor's house. Everyone was there. Grammy reached forward and gave Tommy one of her signature squeezes. "I love you so much, so much . . ." Unconditional love, Tom remembered, is what Grammy had.

"You were a good kid, Thomas, that's why she loved you so much," Ollie reminded him.

"Oh my gosh, it's Uncle Jack, Uncle Michael, Aunt Sara, and Aunt Mary. It's been forever since I've seen them." Uncle Jack was maimed in Vietnam. He had saved his platoon by risking his life during a surprise ambush. Tom recalled as a boy seeing Uncle Jack's medals including the Purple Heart treated as though they were loose change in the top drawer of Jack's dresser. Uncle Jack, just like many others, did not really discuss too much about the war.

Friends and family gave him the respect not to inquire about his experiences. Tom's mother did tell him once that late in the night when she and Uncle Jack had more than a few drinks, he made a comment that she never forgot. As she explained it, he blurted out in a dry and almost guilty manner that he was never so good at something he hated so much.

"Donovan's naked!" yelled Sara. Everyone turned to see what was going on. Young Donovan, the baby of the family, was running on the back lawn as naked as a jay bird, carefree and smiling. Everyone laughed at the sight. He had a bubble blower in his hand and proceeded to run his tan little body around, preventing his sisters and neighbor kids from smacking his "little bottom."

"I remember this. It was Grammy's birthday." It was 1968, right before Uncle Jack went over. Everyone's hair was long, even the kids. Dad had those classic mutton chop sideburns and a bandito mustache. Yet looking even closer, anyone with experience could see that Dad began to have a familiar look in his eyes.

"Tommy cover up your brother," he slurred with a strong Irish brogue.

"They're only having fun, Dad."

Suddenly, his father, as Tom remembered him, was back. He reached his hand over and grabbed Tommy by the hair as if his son had spit in his face and went on, "You do what I say or you'll be eating my foot." His accent always became more pronounced when he decided to indulge himself in beer and anger.

Yeah, this is the old man Tom knew and loved. Those cool mutton chops don't look so cool after the seventh Schlitz. Everyone stopped and looked at Dad. "Tim please, this is Mom's birthday," Mom tried to calm him down.

"You're blaming me for your son not listening to me? I don't need this!" With that, he marched out the front door, but not before grabbing another six-pack of Milwaukee's finest. My uncles tried to calm him and downplay the incident. Grammy and Grandpa were outside and missed this one.

But Tom's family all knew that the extended family did not have to see these incidents as often as they did. His temper would flare at the drop of the hat. "Irish temper," people would casually explain. "Irish curse," I would usually respond. Mom would always tell us how hard it was for him in his early years. Yet it didn't seem to wipe away the brash comments or violent acts.

"Ollie, if you're trying to show me all the good things in my life, you're starting to scare me." Ollie's expression looked as if he was trying to make a point with this latest of visits into my past.

He simply said, "It's amazing that someone who was a victim of an alcoholic would pick that baton up and carry it like a pro."

"The Irish curse," Tom replied.

"That's a cop-out." Tom was still amazed that old Ollie knew the popular come-backs, being some sort of an angel and all.

"What is this, tough love? I'm the one who told you that I was a screw-up. What's the point?"

"You made the choice to stray, Thomas. You had everything going for you. The Father gave you a wonderful family and the talents to do anything you wanted in life. Unfortunately, you followed the crowd instead of using your leadership qualities and set the course."

Tom looked at Ollie, waiting for him to finish his sentence and said "As you know I was not the best leader for my family." Tom stopped, looked up at Ollie and added, "but I must say there are those who thought of me as a powerful businessman."

"Really, Tom, and you believe what you are saying to me?"

Tom looked up at Ollie again with a confident expression; his old ego had emerged, especially when it came to discussing work ethics. His cherished career had meant so much to him.

"Yes, Ollie, and no one showed me otherwise. You saw my father; all he cared about was where he was going to get his next drink," Tom hesitantly fired back, with a little uneasiness in his voice.

"Well then, let us go and revisit your precious career and see how *you* were as a father."

Tom knew he was setting himself up, but could not back down when someone challenged him on his performance at work.

"By the way Mr. Sullivan, performance is measured in a lot of different ways," Ollie said with a little irritation.

As Tom's father walked out of the front door

of Grammy's house, they followed but traveled to a different place.

"Now, let's move forward in your past a little, and take us to a time when you were the age your father was at your Grammy's house."

"Alright, I guess, where will we go?"

"Just sit back and observe."

At that they whisked along through another fog and stopped in what seemed to be a large conference room. It was in fact one of Tom's old company meeting rooms. Tom saw himself in his mid-thirties, and the same age his father was. Tom was sitting at a large conference table, surrounded by all his old company "cohorts."

I was at the height of my career at this age, he thought to himself. "I was the account manager for one of the company's largest accounts in the software business," Tom reminded Ollie.

Tom remembered how he was in a very powerful position back then. He had a budget in the millions to handle business and keep customers happy. He had to entertain with whatever it took, to move the needle in terms of sales. Some buyers, as Tom recalled, were not as greedy as others.

Looking around the room, he saw his old Vice President, Mr. Roberts and the Director of Sales, Mr. Welch. He remembered how he originally disliked their way of doing business, but then later he had adjusted and conformed. They had no scruples and would say or do anything to get what they needed. They would also fire anyone at will and would motivate with fear.

"Mr. Sullivan," the vice president spoke up, "and how do you propose to achieve your forecast?"

Tom used to enjoy taking on the management. "Well, as you know, sir, my forecast is an objective where I am paid a bonus, so I intend to give my customers 'an offer they cannot refuse.'" Young Tom knew he could make such a vague response, since he was well above exceeding his sales objectives for the year. He knew Roberts was not after him that day.

Mr. Roberts smirked, and the rest of the room, noticing the Vice President's approval, burst into laughter.

"Well Mr. Sullivan, try not to put whatever you commit to in writing."

"I most definitely will not."

Not satisfied until he's made someone squirm, Roberts turned to his weakest manager.

"Jenkins."

"Ah, Yes Sir, Mr. Roberts," Jenkins said uneasily.

"Every manger in our division is achieving at least 110% of their objectives. Sullivan alone is at

120%, so I allow him to make such statements, yet you are only at 90%. Why is that?"

Jenkins fidgeted and turned to look for support from the director as Roberts addressed him. He looked at his old friend Sully, who just shrugged his shoulders.

"Mr. Roberts, I think Mr. Welch will agree my sales are going quite well considering what I have had to overcome this year."

Jenkins looked at Mr. Welch for some kind of support, but Welch just sat there with a stern look on his face without acknowledging a word.

Jenkins continued, "As everyone knows my second largest account went into bankruptcy this year, and I had to find business elsewhere to make up for the lost sales."

Roberts and Welch returned looks of disapproval at each other.

Roberts spoke up as Jenkins paused, "If you knew one thing about bankruptcy or forecasting, you might have seen the signals far in advance. I will not listen to these excuses."

The different department heads sensed that Roberts was in one of his moods, and had found a victim to take it out on. Everyone lowered their heads, not as low as Jenkins though. He knew the beating was not over; it had just begun.

"You see Mr. Jenkins we are in business to make money. We build the finest software solutions in the industry, and thus, deserve a premium for it. What I mean by premium is not only in terms of profit, but also people. We are not in business to subsidize your incompetence. We are in business for the stockholders to make money. I *will* make my budget this year, and whoever does not help me will pay dearly. Do you understand me?"

"Yes sir, I do."

"That's good, Jenkins."

With that, Roberts and Welch both paused, and stared at everyone in the room.

Tom remembered these fear tactics they used to motivate their troops. Tom was the youngest one in the room and had no fear whatsoever. He had their number. They thought they were so superior, until the day would come when they would be replaced. So he learned the system and would say what they wanted to hear, but he would not crawl for them.

"This concludes our budget meeting. Get back to work and make us proud, gentlemen."

One of Tom's old buddies turned to him and said, "Hey, I guess congratulations are in order."

Tom replied, "What, I haven't made my numbers yet; I have two more months to go."

"Sully, no, didn't your wife have a baby last night?"

"Oh yeah, thanks Bill." Tom answered, as he couldn't stop wondering why they had called this meeting.

Maybe they're going to get rid of Jenkins. He is worthless. I could turn those accounts around and make a lot more money. Tom continued to think rather than listen to his friend.

"How is Tammy doing?"

"Oh, she is doing fine; she is a real trooper."

Tom looked at both Roberts and Welch, and tried to figure out what they were saying to each other.

"Well, what is it Tom?"

"What's what, Bill?"

"Your baby; is it a boy or a girl?"

"Girl, I'm sorry, yeah, our first girl, we named her Susan; thanks for asking."

Thomas had enough. "Can we leave now, Ollie?" He said in disgust, remembering how he used to be.

"Your 30's were not your best years. But up until then, you were on the right track. You seem to forget how you studied The Word. You tried to help the less fortunate. You cared for your fellow man.

Then it seemed later in life you put more effort into 'chasing the buck and the skirt.'"

Tom listened intently but was still amazed at the choice of words he was using. "Ollie, did you say, 'chasing the skirt'? How does an angel know what that is?"

Ollie smirked and replied, "I've seen and heard everything before your ancestors knew the luxury of what chasing the buck or skirt was. We want to help you."

"I'm an old man Ollie, it's too late."

"Ye of so little faith, who do you think you're talking to?" Ollie raised his voice. "If we thought it was necessary we could take you back to the time when nomadic tribes invaded Europe. We can change anything," Ollie reminded him impatiently. Tom paused. An old archive of a thought struck him like a bolt of lighting. But fear also set in as he found it hard to have a request.

"Wait, it's not like . . ." Tom paused again.

"It's not like what? Say it, Thomas." He looked up directly at Ollie in fear. It had been so long since he had any thought of hope. It wasn't a simple thing to conjure up. Years in prison teach you to not dream or hope. It will drive you insane. He finally thought of the letter, thought of Tammy, thought of the kids, and thought about Scotty.

He then forced out air hard with a low coarse voice, "Could I have another chance at life?"

Ollie looked straight back into Tom's eyes and simply said, "It can be done."

Tom was seized with an emotion he could not remember having. He had a mix of hope and excitement but mostly fear. "Wait, wait, what are we talking about here?"

"We are talking about what you just asked me," Ollie replied.

"Just a second, I don't think I'm ready quite yet," Tom muttered. "How will it work? What about Little Ronnie Becker?"

"Ronnie is and will be fine."

"What about Tammy, and the kids?"

"They will love you as they did before you abused them."

Tom did a double take at Ollie, but understood what he was trying to convey. "Okay. . . okay. . . wait . . . I'm an old, abused, feeble man."

"Tom we will take care of all that. Now do you want this or not?"

"Yes . . . please . . . another chance. Yes, with all my heart."

Tom came close enough for the request to be granted. "All right then, good, but there is something I must say. You won't remember what happened to you. And when we send you back, you will still have your drinking problems. You will be just as vulnerable, and you still must turn your life around."

Tom's gleam of hope began to diminish. "Oh," Tom hesitantly answered. "Does it have to be that way?"

"Don't worry; I will be there with you. There is another thing Tom. You cannot commit another mortal sin."

"I won't, believe me, I won't."

"This is out of my control, but if you do commit another mortal sin, we will have to bring you back to where you were in prison. We are giving you a chance to do it again, and do it the way you have always prayed about. Remember, when you were just put away, and you prayed so hard for another chance to do things right."

Tom remembered. He prayed nonstop for a couple of months in the beginning. Day and night, begging God to give him a second chance. He hardly ate or slept for months. He started to lose his mind and then slowly gave up and conformed to the prison way of life.

"Tom, do it right this time. It will not be easy. You have a lot to make up, a lot of mending to do."

"So I won't remember anything?"

Ollie looked down at his feet and then replied "Yes, that is right Tom."

"Okay Ollie, I trust you, and I will do my best."

From out of nowhere a wind developed and Ollie seemed to move away. "But what if . . ."

"I'm sorry those are the rules. God be with you, Thomas, we love you."

"But Ollie . . . what about . . ."

"God be with you."

Chapter 4

All of a sudden, things began to happen. Tom could feel himself traveling fast, but he could not see. He felt cold and warm winds rush past him. Flashes of light would come and go. Then just as it began, it ended, and he felt himself falling.

It was a beautiful spring day in the Carolinas and Tom was doing his favorite workout, running outside in his neighborhood. *Oh my God, thank you God, thank you Ollie,* thought Tom. *I feel alive again. No pain, strong and alive. I'm here. Look at me; I'm strong. I'm young again. I'm running my old three-mile run. Dear God, look at my legs. I'm running fast and strong.*

Suddenly an SUV slowed down and a young woman yelled out, "Hey buddy, don't work out too much. Leave some energy for Marta's party tonight." Tom vaguely remembered her. That's right, we were close with them. Cindy, Cindy Harris, he thought to himself. She's treating me like I'm somebody.

"Sure," he replied. She smiled and drove off.

Tom thought—I'm really here. I'm only about ½ mile from the old house, that beautiful old house. How can this be happening? All Tom could think about was Tammy and the kids. He ran like a sprinter down the hill, over the creek, across the bridge and into the neighborhood.

Another car pulled in honking the horn. "You're a stud muffin, Sullivan!" It was old Ray Harris. Tom waved, and then ran onto the front lawn of his house. He even instinctively slapped the mailbox, as he used to do many years ago after a nice run.

"Tom," yelled a familiar voice across the street. "You need to talk to Trey and get him to run with you."

"Yeah, sure, see you." Tom could not believe he was back at home. And then it hit him as he saw the Suburban. He stopped in his tracks. Tammy sold it after the accident. Ollie said it didn't happen. *I'm not supposed to be remembering this.* He began to feel a wave of fear.

Please don't let this be a dream. I've got to see my kids. I've got to get to the front door.

He made an attempt to move very slowly so as not to disturb his sleep.

Please God, let this be real.

He walked slowly up the driveway. He could see himself in the reflection of the truck windows.

Look at me, the wrinkles are gone, and my hair is back. My eyes are clear and wide open like they used to be.

"Please stay with me, Ollie" he whispered. Tom approached the front door slowly. He could not believe what was going on. He could feel someone pushing him toward the door. "Here it goes," he said as he opened the door.

It all came back to him. His arm and leg hairs were standing on end. His heart was pounding a mile a minute. He was still awake. All his senses were keen and alert. It was like yesterday. He slowly opened the front door. He felt like he was somehow intruding. The furniture was just as he remembered. I never appreciated this big, old beautiful house. He was always on the run, always chasing that buzz or buck. He could hear kids playing upstairs. There was an aroma of something wonderful cooking in the kitchen. "Hey babe, how was the run?"

"Tammy?" He said in a startled, choked-up voice. She came from around the corner. She looked so beautiful and so young. He had forgotten how cute her figure was. She was wearing those shorts that he always liked. Her hair was blond and cut short.

"Hey Tom, try this," as she held up a spoonful of chili for him to taste. Tom could not open his mouth. He just stared with his eyes wide open. "Open your mouth, silly, not your eyes."

Her eyes were the signature knockout feature about her—so wide open and beautiful, almost a touch of Asian in them. I never told her enough how beautiful she was, Tom thought. Tom could hardly move. All he could muster to say was "I'm sorry honey."

"About what? You're not late." Tammy kissed him on the lips. It felt so good. "What's wrong?"

"Nothing, everything's great, babe." The words just came out. He hadn't said that to her in over thirty years. "I love you so much," Tom said.

"I love you too. Are you sure you're okay? I told you not to run so hard. You're 42 not 30." *I'm 42,* he thought to himself in amazement.

"Where are the kids?"

"The girls are upstairs. Scotty's at Daniel's house."

Tom ran upstairs yelling "Hey girls!"

"Hi Daddy!"

"Daddy, Susan won't let me play with her Barbie."

"Come here sweetie; give me a big hug." Little Rachael was only 3 years old but would always give her daddy a hug on command. "I love you so much sweetie."

"Daddy," Susan ran to get in the action. "Hug me too, Daddy."

"Both of you hug me." Tom was overwhelmed with emotion. "I love you both so much."

"I love you too, Daddy," they both said in unison. "Come see our hideout in the play room."

"Sure, sweetie." It was becoming too much for Tom. He dropped to his knees and his eye's swelled up.

"What's wrong, Daddy?"

"Nothing sweetie, I'm fine."

"Get up, Daddy."

Tom could not believe that he was actually talking to his two baby girls. He had been given a second chance. He was younger. His kids were younger. Tammy was absolutely beautiful, and she loved him again. He was so afraid that he would wake up or do something wrong. He felt like sobbing but had to control himself.

Just then the front door opened and closed with a slam. "Hey Mom, can I go to the lake with Daniel tomorrow? His dad just bought a boat." It was Scotty. Tom jumped up to his feet and began to run down the stairs.

Tammy responded, "Honey, I don't think so, we're going to a party tonight and we'll be up late."

Tom leaped down the last few steps and

landed in front of his son. Scotty stood to attention, a little startled by his father's exertion.

"Sorry Dad, I didn't mean to slam the door." Tom reached down to give him a big hug. Scotty had not been given a hug of this sort from his father since he was a toddler.

"I love you so much buddy; I love you so much. I'm so proud of you."

Tammy walked slowly from around the corner to view what she had been hearing. "Dad, you're squeezing me, I can't breathe." Tammy and Scotty looked at each other questioning the passionate mood Dad was exhibiting.

Tom put his hands on his son's shoulders and faced him with tears in his eyes and a smile on his face. "How are you doing, Son?"

"I'm fine Dad. Is something wrong?"

"No, everything is great. We need to spend more time together. Hey I know, how about if I take you and your friends to the lake tomorrow?"

"Dad thanks, but we don't have a boat."

"So we'll rent one. Meet me right here tomorrow morning at 8:00."

Scotty's eyes opened wide with surprise. "Alright Dad, you're on. Can I go and tell my friends?"

"Sure, tell anyone you want."

The front door slammed again as he left his father in the foyer. Tammy looked over with a genuine smile of approval. She could not detect him slurring, so she was happy that Tom seemed sober with his promise.

Tom began to settle down but tried to think where he was in time with relation to the accident.

What day is it? A party with the neighbors? It was always a common occurrence to have a neighborhood party. She will think I'm crazy if I ask what the date is.

"Tammy, where is the newspaper?"

"I don't know," she said defensively.

Oh, this used to be a sore subject with me, Tom remembered. *I used to lose it over this.*

She said nothing, waiting for the blow. He did not feel the anger but did start to feel nervous and anxious.

"Please go get ready for tonight, honey," Tammy said. Tom's wife sensed she had dodged a bullet, or maybe she was protected by the effects of his run.

He looked in the kitchen and stopped to look out the back door. Everything was beautiful. He walked outside onto the screened porch. This place was great. How could he have thrown all this away? There it was, *The Charlotte Observer.* Tom's anxiety went up about 100 beats as he read the date at the top of the newspaper. Friday, May 18th, 2001. He just stared at it in disbelief.

They brought me back to the day it all happened. I need more time.

Now he really started to begin to feel fear. He started to have an incredible urge for a drink, just a couple of beers. It had been forever.

No . . . I'm not supposed to remember all this. What happens if my memory goes away?

"Oliver, why is Thomas remembering the past?" asked an angel who was overseeing the transformation with Ollie. Ollie did not reply. "Oliver, please answer me. Why is Mr. Sullivan having recollection?"

"How is he supposed to change if he does not remember what he needs to change?" Ollie replied.

"We can guide him, Ollie."

"What about Hugh Richardson? He only lasted a couple of hours."

"Hugh was tempted without listening to our message. Make the change, Oliver."

The front door swung open. "Hey, you guys, don't forget to bring the Coronas tonight," said Cindy, an old friend and neighbor. Tom jumped to his feet.

"Yeah, and tell Jeff to bring the Grey Goose

and I'll bring the limes. Those Blue Meanies won't have a chance."

The words just rolled off his lips. Tammy and Cindy laughed and rolled their eyes. Tom all of a sudden had a brief spell of amnesia, forgetting what he had said to make them laugh. The emotion of guilt began to mix in with Tom's thoughts. "Wait, I mean I don't know. Maybe we should rethink what we're doing tonight, Tammy."

"What do you mean?" Tammy asked.

"Yeah," said Cindy.

"Everything's all planned. It's going to be a great party. Bill and Leslie will be there, Alan and Laurie, Sheila and Rick. We all have babysitters, a rare occasion," Cindy mentioned with a little sarcasm.

Tammy turned her wonder into more of an accusing expression. "If you think you and the guys are going to Vinney's Tavern again and then show up halfway through the evening, you have another thing coming."

"No, no it's not that at all. No, I'm just thinking we always do the same thing." Tom continued as his guilt did not let up. "We always go out and treat the event like it is the last party of the century." I was the worst to blame on this, he thought to himself. "We basically talk about the same things and maybe mix it up a little. We flirt with each other. We tell everyone how great we are, and then we go home late in the evening. Tomorrow, we will wake up, try to act as if we are doing just great, and make the kids pay for our abuse."

Cindy turns to Tammy with a confused look. "I think you might be exaggerating just a little," Tammy spoke up.

"Why should I feel guilty for having a good time?" Cindy rebutted, sensing Tom's anguish. "I don't know what you've got up your sleeve, but you and my husband are sticking with us tonight," Cindy went on.

"Yeah, relax. You're acting strange," Tammy jumped in again.

"Well, twenty years from now our livers and kidneys will thank us," Tom reminded them. They both looked at him inquisitively. They thought he was trying to pull something or just mess with them for amusement. There was no reason for them to think otherwise. He used to pull pranks at the drop of a hat. He was the life of the party and needed to be the center of attention. This can't be a dream; it is all too real—he convinced and comforted himself.

The two women ignored him and began to talk about preparations. Then Tammy looked up and said, "Tom, please go upstairs and get ready for tonight."

Chapter 5

Tom suddenly froze with fear. Upstairs in the foyer, out the large window were two young boys playing outside. He barely spoke the words in a whisper, "Little Ronnie." Little Ronnie, as everyone referred to him, was riding his Big Wheel as he always did up and down the driveway in front of his house.

Tom felt strong emotions, which began to affect him now. "I did not do it," he said to himself. "I'm not going to do it." He could not allow himself to visualize the accident, or he would get sick as he had done so many times in the past. He started to lose it and ran down the stairs, out the door and across the street to see the young boy. Tammy and Cindy noticed the activity and followed behind him out into the front yard. The exertion must have snapped his emotional state into shape as he approached the young boy.

Ronnie always had a natural smile. "Hi, Mr. Sullivan."

"Hey buddy, you doing okay?" Ronnie just looked up and smirked.

"Yes Mr. Sullivan." Tom felt the sensation that he knew something.

As Tom turned around he saw Scotty doing what he always did back then, playing some kind of game or sport with someone. In this case, he was throwing a baseball across the street to Daniel as he went home. "Hey Dad," he yelled nonchalantly.

"Darn it Scotty, how many times do I have to tell you not to throw the ball across the street when cars are coming?"

Scotty dropped his head and said, "Okay Dad, I'm sorry."

Something had happened. Tom felt different. He all of a sudden felt a pain for acting that way to his boy but did not know why. He could see the disappointment in Tammy's eyes 40 yards away. "Scotty, don't worry about it. Hey, sport, just stay out of the street."

"Tom, you're coming tonight, right?" A man yelled from Little Ronnie's front yard. It was Ron Sr. Last time Tom saw him, he was being sentenced.

"Hey, yeah, sure I'll be there."

"Maybe we can break away and head over to Vinney's." A sharp pain hit Tom's gut.

"Yeah sure, we'll see."

"Okay tiger, leave Mr. Sullivan alone, let's

get inside and get ready for dinner," Ronnie's dad said to his son.

"Is Tina babysitting tonight, Dad?" Little Ronnie asked.

"Yes, now go inside."

"Hey Tom," Ron Sr. said, "Hold up. I know we've talked about this before, but what are your thoughts about putting in some speed bumps on this street?" Tom suddenly stopped and paused, again not knowing why.

Noticing this Ron Sr. asked, "What's up, man? Are you okay?"

"No nothing, I ah . . . , I'm just getting this deja vu feeling." Tom had remembered how they had coincidently discussed speed bumps for the kids and how they used to curse the drivers who sped down the road looking to exit the neighborhood. The worst were the pizza delivery guys. The neighborhood parents would take a stand and yell out to the drivers to slow . . . down. . . . Although the neighbors thought amongst themselves that Ron and Wendy were crazy to let Ronnie drive that toy down the driveway. After the accident no one said a word about it. If you are drinking, the fault goes nowhere but to the person behind the wheel.

Last time Tom had seen Ron was at the trial. Understandably, Ron could not even look Tom in the eyes. It physically hurt Tom to be in the same room with him. He even fantasized that Ron would pull out a gun and help put him out of his misery. It would have been understandable. Tom could not look at himself in any kind of reflection. He was so full of disgust.

What really drove him crazy was that he was boldly against drinking and driving. He never did it. He would drink too much on occasion, but he never got behind the wheel. He and Tammy both felt adamant about this. Tom also was one of those people who, after drinking too many, had a tendency to lose all memory. He would usually ask friends or Tammy to make sure he acted appropriately. Tammy was not proud of how he would just transform himself into an uncontrollable drinker. She would basically convey to him in so many words how he diminished what people thought of him. Tom realized that she was losing respect for him. He was also transforming her into an enabler.

"Hey partner, get out of the road or you will become a speed bump yourself," yelled Ron. Snapping out of it, Tom looked up from staring down at his feet, waved his arm behind him, then finished crossing the street. He looked up at the sky as he made it to the sidewalk. This is a beautiful day, he thought to himself. As he walked toward his house he looked up across the neighborhood and found solace in those thick wooded pine trees. Those pines were always so inviting and tranquil. At least that is what people used to tell him, and they were right.

How long is Ollie going to let me remember my past? I seem to be going in and out of my memories. How am I going to function without my guard up?

As he approached, he was still in awe of what he had as a young man. Tammy was working in the garden that she so enjoyed. "Daddy, push me on the swing, please," yelled Rachel from the backyard.

"No, Rachel, leave Daddy alone, he needs to take a shower and get ready for tonight." Tammy would always chime in at Tom's defense about having to do the "daddy thing." Tom looked over at her as she was finishing her sentence. Rachel did not even try for a rebuttal and began to pull dandelions from the backyard. Tammy just shrugged her shoulders as if to apologize and went back to gardening.

Had it gotten this bad? I did not have time to push my baby on the swing, and I had everyone accustomed to this way of life.

Tom walked over towards the backyard. He pushed the side gate, which took a little strength, as the bottom was rubbing against the Carolina red clay. He approached Rachel. She looked up with a pure, genuine smile, showing her baby teeth. "Come on honey, let me push you."

"Yeah, thanks Daddy!" she screamed. At that, Tom picked his baby girl up. She was as light as a doll, only being 3 years old and a little small at that.

"Now let's see, which one do you want to sit on?" Tom asked Rachel.

"It doesn't matter, Daddy."

As he gently placed her on the flexible green plastic seat he asked, "Now how high do you want to go?"

"As high as the trees, Daddy!" With that Tom pulled her back ever so slightly and released her carefully. He looked over at those pines. They were tall and beautiful giving the feeling of protection from the outside world. This was our home, our bedroom community. Rachel laughed with joy at every push.

Tom never remembered her enjoying her father so much. She giggled uncontrollably. It was all so surreal. It was like she knew something. As if it was a test. A test for me, and she was enjoying her dad again and knew it was not going to last. She, of all the children, had the least time with me. She didn't get a chance to have many good memories.

Tom panned across the backyard and admired the landscaping that Tammy had spent so much time working at. He hated this kind of work, but she enjoyed it so much. He kept looking across and fixed his sights on the house he was so proud of. It was the largest house he ever had, and he bought it new. His parents never even had a new house. The screen porch was an excellent addition, but the best part was that it was built with his own hands—with a lot of help from a neighborhood "fix it" friend.

We did have a lot of good memories in this place.

"Ollie, this is enough. Thomas is obviously still enjoying the fortunes of his memories. We had an agreement on this, and I gave my approval when you came to me regarding Mr. Sullivan."

"All right," Ollie said "I just wanted him to have some time during his transformation."

Suddenly, Tom stopped in his tracks. Rachel's swing landed into his arms. "High as the trees, Daddy!"

Tom looked down at his watch for the first time. "All right honey, that was great, Daddy needs to do some work." With that, he walked quickly towards the house. He did not know what it was, but something was different. All of a sudden, he remembered that he had to give a big presentation next week. He also had not checked his cell phone for messages since before he began his run.

It was 3:00 P.M. on a Friday. Most of his colleagues start winding down at 1:00 P.M. if they worked in the field, but not Tom. Work was his number-one priority. Although he did not realize that his drinking took from his work, his family, and his life. There were only so many hours in a day, and just because you put 60 or 70 hours in a week does not mean you are productive.

As Tom walked into the back of the house, his mind became engorged with a million thoughts. They came at him in all directions, as if a flood gate had just opened up. He walked into the back through his screened porch and had to stop to lean against one of the chairs. His head was pounding and he began to overheat. Everything was hitting him at once and he never had so many conflicting thoughts race into his mind.

Where am I standing in regards to this month's sales quota? How are Tammy and the kids doing? What time does the party start tonight? Do I have enough Grey Goose for the evening? Who is babysitting tonight? Why are we going out? I miss the kids.

His heart started to pound hard, and he began to feel faint.

Where is my cell phone? What have I been doing all day?

Questions continued to plague him. Tom

never felt this way before. Stress was never an issue for Tom, or so he thought. He was a pro at stress management, considering all the balls he had been juggling for years. This was different, however; these thoughts and questions were not one-dimensional. They were conflicting thoughts and questions. He had an overbearing conscience with a counteracting thought that arose and stopped him as he tried to move forward. He bent over in pain and began to breathe heavily. "I'm not hung over," he thought to himself. "What did I do last night?"

Tammy had been watching him through the family room and slowly stepped out onto the porch entrance. "Tom, what is wrong?" Her presence soothed him.

"I don't know. I think I'm having an anxiety attack or something."

"See, I told you not to push it too hard on your run. You're not 30 anymore."

As he heard her words, thoughts began to rush in.

Why is she attacking me? I love her so much. This stress is on me because of her and the family. I love my kids. I can't do anything right for her.

"I'm okay, I just need to catch my breath," he whispered back to Tammy.

"You're going out tonight, right?" she questioned Tom.

"Sure, but I'm not going to blow it out." She looked at him in amazement. Those were not common words coming from Tom. It was vice versa; these were the preaching words usually coming from Tammy.

"Where is Scotty?"

"He is upstairs playing videos games with Daniel."

"Who is watching the kids tonight?"

"They're going over to Bill and Leslie's house and being watched by Becky. What is it with all the questions, Tom?" she fired back at him.

"No, nothing I just miss the kids, that's all. Do you really want to go out tonight, Tammy?"

All of a sudden she began to get angry. "What is this, have you already been drinking today? What are you hiding from me?" Tammy always had reason to believe that something was up with him. He usually had something up his sleeve.

Tom wondered why she was so defensive. "Okay, okay, we'll go out." As Tom finished his sentence, the cell phone rang. It was in the kitchen on top of the fridge. He leaped forward to catch it. The number flashed across the lit screen, but Tom didn't recognize the number. "Sullivan," Tom blurted out in a business manner.

"Hey, buddy, I'm here with Adam. We just finished 18 holes and are having some beers at Vinney's Tavern. Come on down!" It was Al, his next-door neighbor.

"Hey man, no, I can't. We're just getting ready for tonight." There was a short pause on the other side of the line.

"Are you kidding me? I thought we were meeting here first."

"Sorry, man, a couple of things came up, see you tonight." With that Tom had to remember how to turn off the cell phone and wondered why he was confused at this. Tammy, on the other hand, was staring at him.

"You can go if you want."

Why does she want me to go?

"I thought you would be happy if I didn't," Tom said.

"No, the point is you're not happy unless you go. So why put me through your grief."

Tom started to feel an uncontrollable anger build up. The expression on his face did not hide his feelings and Tammy stepped back. But just as it arose he was able to cool it down. "Let's just relax and get ready," he suggested.

Tom walked upstairs and looked for the kids. "Susan, where are you?" Tom felt an urge to stay with the kids.

"Daddy, I'm up in my room. We're going over to Amy's house tonight." He stepped into her room and found her doing what she always did in her spare time, drawing pictures.

"That's great sweetie." Then he went into his bedroom to get ready. Something was missing, maybe in a good way. He did not have that anxious feeling. That excited feeling which made going to a party fun. That energy he normally got anticipating the buzz, the flirting and the joking.

As he dried off from the shower, he stopped and admired his physique and appearance in the mirror. He also took a mental note that he needed to not be so vain.

"Sorry for those comments," Tammy said, handing Tom a cold Corona. Tom instinctively put his hand out, but did not immediately have a swig, as was the usual next move. "I'm glad you didn't go to Vinney's. Try to keep it light on the vodka tonight." As Tom was deciding what to wear, Tammy went back downstairs.

Tom could hear Tammy talking on the phone. He hurried and picked out some of his favorite party wear, and headed down. Tammy was not on the phone; instead she was entertaining Rick, a family friend who had stopped by. They both finished up their conversation then turned around to acknowledge Tom with two huge welcoming smiles. "Hey, you're already dressed," Tammy said as she turned towards Tom.

"Hey Rick, where's Shelia?" Rick, Shelia and their kids were old family friends.

Tammy was very close with Shelia, but had recently become close with Rick as well. Tom kind of understood since he was close with Cindy, especially during the wee hours in the morning of a late party. "Well, as I was just telling Tammy, I'm in the dog house again." He and Tammy both exchanged knowing smiles.

"Really," Tom acknowledged.

"Yes, it seems that old Ricky played golf all day then decided to stay at the 19th hole all night." Tammy always found it humorous when someone else's husband got in trouble.

"I forgot that Shelia's parents had arrived last night and I failed to make it on time for dinner."

"Tammy you should not get between Shelia and Rick's issues."

Tammy smiled from ear to ear and responded, "I'm just listening."

"Well, I have to go before the warden keeps

me in lockdown for the night. See you guys later." With that Rick darted out to his "944," which was still running in the driveway.

"Okay, the kids are already at Bill and Leslie's house. I'll be ready in a few." With that, Tammy ran upstairs with a Corona in hand. Tom could see the kids playing across the street. A car sped by and Tom conjured up his usual anger at the driver. He turned on the TV and flipped through the channels just to kill time. The phone rang and Tom answered it. "Hey buddy, you guys coming down?" It was Jeff.

"Don't worry, we'll be there, Tammy is just getting ready."

"Hey bud, don't forget the Goose Juice." Tom had to think twice where they kept it. He opened the cupboard above the oven, and there it was, a new two-liter bottle.

"Looks like you're in luck, my man."

"You mean we're both in luck. Now tell Tammy to hurry her cute little self." Tom could hear Tammy using the hair dryer. He reached up to grab the premium vodka, but as he clutched the bottle his hands began to shake.

Tom could still see the kids playing outside and told himself to take it easy tonight. The only problem was saying this to himself was a nice thought for the moment, yet it usually never came to fruition. The problem was he tended to "kick it in" a little heavier if someone tried to slow him down.

He started to open the Grey Goose, but instead put it on the counter and reached in the fridge to grab a cold Corona. He had left the first one upstairs untouched. Again his hands began to shake as he quickly opened it and took a nice long swig. The first swig of the evening was always the best. He never remembered it tasting so good. All of a sudden, he felt as if he had done something wrong. Tammy came from around the corner with an excited look on her face. She had that energy that one gets before a party, and she was beaming.

"How about a cold one, baby," Tammy said in her flirtatious way.

"Damn it, Tammy! Where are the limes?" Her smile went south as she handed him the bag of limes from the refrigerator. He caught himself attacking Tammy for no reason and felt stupid about it. As she brushed by him, Tom could not help himself from admiring the allure of her. She smelled great and was wearing a nice tight short skirt. She was well tanned and her legs were superb for a woman of her age with three kids. Tom had always appreciated how she did not realize her beauty.

Tammy looked over at the Grey Goose on the counter and shook her head in an unfavorable manner. If he just had a couple of vodkas, she would not say a thing. But it was always too extreme when it came to that stuff. It might as well have been a drug, she would complain to her friends. Tom caught her look and simply said "Don't worry, I'll take it easy."

"Whatever," Tammy replied. Yet Tom's late night binges with the boys allowed Tammy to get to know the neighbors a little more intimately. The wives would often share their marital problems with each other. But the problems were not all on the same level. Not everyone had alcoholic husbands.

The drinking husbands joked and named their late night adventures "the 7th inning." The non-alcoholic guys would actually wonder in awe how those guys could leave their beautiful wives for the evening. The amazing thing was Tom had been naive enough to believe that all his fellow neighbors lived under the same brotherhood code. Among other unwritten laws, number one was, you can flirt, but don't entertain any thoughts of greener pastures. Tom had always known to never even discuss any type of romantic experience he had with his wife. Number one it was disrespectful to his wife, but the main reason was not to give anyone a mental picture of his personal experiences. He had grown up a Catholic boy and understood to never "kiss and tell." There was a reason for this rule, and

Tom understood not to give anyone insider information.

One thing Tom had going for him was that Tammy just did not have it in her. That was one of the reasons he married her. He could trust her. "Okay, let's get going," Tom announced as he clutched the bottle. He grabbed the keys then abruptly stopped to stare at them. "Hey, why don't we just walk there?"

Tammy took some sort of appetizer out of the refrigerator, hesitated and said, "No, let's take the truck. We have a few things to bring to the party. Don't worry, if I have more than three beers, we'll just walk home." That was the normal procedure to drive down and walk home. She did not say if "you only have three" because that was never an option.

Chapter 6

The Sullivans were fashionably late, as usual. Marta had planned extensively for this event. You could hear the band playing in the backyard, so they walked around through the side gate. Everyone was already there and grouped in their places to settle for the evening. "The Goose Master," yelled Jeff as he caught sight of Tom. Five or six fellows chimed in repeatedly "Goose, Goose, Goose, Goose." It was an awesome night; the weather was cooperating with a warm spring breeze. Everyone was there: Alan and Laurie, Jeff and Cindy, Rick and Shelia, and so on. Adam, who came alone, always had some sort of story to tell. He and Tom exchanged nods as he was finishing one of his many humorous tales. The neighborhood was relatively new at only 5 years old. Most of the occupants were young families and upper-middle-class climbers.

It was John's 35th birthday, so Marta went all-out with a Mariachi band and a margarita machine to boot. There were a lot of people there, and everyone had settled into their cliques. Tom never let that stop him. This was his arena; he was a pro. He would slowly work the crowd and jump from one group to the next at his leisure. Along the way, he would promote his Goose Juice, and make sure everyone was having a great time. It came naturally for him, not as if he had an agenda. His only agenda was for everyone to like him and to have a great time. But in order for Tom to have a great time, he needed alcohol, lots of it.

Tammy used to remind him that it was not the "party of the century," but it was hard not to feel this way. Tom loved it when the party would dwindle down to just the serious drinkers. They would amuse each other with their wit and collectively solve the world's problems into the wee hours of the morning. This was the time that you could "let your hair down" and figure out how to set your course of success.

Tammy headed straight for her close group of friends. Cindy was one of Tom's closest friends and would usually hang out with him in his late-night discussions. Rick, on the other hand, was well thought of by Tammy and would trade jokes and flirts. Tom did not mind except that he and Rick seemed to have backed off a little on their friendship. They might have become friends too quickly and knew a little too much about each other. It didn't help that Shelia and

Tammy were always on the phone comparing notes about their husbands' attributes and faults. Shelia was very good at manipulating any social situation and focused her energy on making Rick the center of all her discussions. This can be a dangerous thing, putting your husband on a pedestal for others to admire.

The evening was progressing to Marta's delight. People began to dance with the rhythm of the band's music. Everyone was scattered about in and out of the house. A few were checking out John's new home theater system and watching a ball game. Tom was having a good time but felt an uncontrollable urge to hold back and not get intoxicated. It was already 9:30 and Tom had been passing around the Goose but had not indulged. He was only on his second Corona, which was amazing for him. As he made his rounds, he kept an eye on Tammy. She would return a smile and seemed to be getting the full use out of the margarita machine.

Time continued to slip away as the party had been a success. Shelia, as she usually did, announced that she had to get home and relieve the babysitter. With that, Tammy and the rest of the group got her to stay a little longer, although they knew it was just a matter of time before she would disappear. Rick, Ron and Bill were passing out cigars and enjoying the ice-cold drinks. When Shelia finally left at 11:00, the structure of the party changed. Cindy made her way over to Tom. Jeff, her husband, had enough as he always did this time of the evening, and went home in a bad mood. With Jeff's departure, the 7th inning had begun. The band had wrapped it up but left behind the drums, the bongos and, worst of all, the microphone.

One would think as the evening progressed things would kind of cool down, but this was not the case in the Stoneyhill neighborhood. The music went up a few notches with the help of some CDs. The dancing and singing was out of control and the drinking was unstoppable. Tom started to enjoy himself. He was dancing with Cindy and grabbed a bottle of water. They both knew it was a harmless relationship. They both had kids, and Tom knew they would never break the code. He looked over and could hear Tammy laughing and making a comment about his dance style.

Suddenly Cindy's cell phone rang and Jeff proceeded to give her the third degree. Cindy looked over at Tom and said "I have to go, but I will be back." She kissed him on the cheek and slipped four cigarettes in his top shirt pocket. With that Tom had lost his buddy. He looked at his bottle of water and began to crave the vodka that he cherished. He felt as if he were doing something wrong and began to miss Tammy and the kids. He told himself this is the last one, but he could not get rid of his overbearing craving for a cigarette. Tom thought this would be the perfect time to be bad and have a "ciggy," something Tammy despised. He reached in his pocket but did not have a lighter. "Tom," yelled Adam "come over here and join us for a cigar."

"I'll be back in a minute," he said as he made his way through the crowd and around to the front of the house. Tom remembered he had a lighter in the truck console. This way he could have a smoke without having a confrontation with Tammy.

Things are going to get better; I am not out of control. I need to grow up and become a spiritual leader for my family. I will finish this drink, be responsible, grab Tammy and walk home. We can pick up the truck tomorrow.

He approached the truck, opened the door and went for the console. The lighter was not in it. He realized that the lighter was at home in the kitchen drawer. All of a sudden a strange sensation came over him. Someone was watching. He looked around and noticed that the windows had been closed. He also started to hear some heavy breathing. Tom felt a chill and slowly turned his head toward the rear of the Suburban. The next vision was a sight that put him in shock. It was surreal, like a slow-motion moment.

There in the back between the captain seats was Tammy embraced with Rick.

For a split second they stayed there as if they were invisible. Tom let out a winded breath in disbelief, but did not utter a word. Then Rick jumped up and started in "Tom, hold up, let's talk." Tom felt intense rage boil inside of him, and he looked down at his keys. He wanted to leave this place and be with his kids. They both quickly climbed out of the truck as Tom stood there clenching his fist. He looked down at his keys and began to climb in. But something came over him.

"Tom, wait," Tammy begged him, "let's just stop." She looked obviously drunk as she slurred her pleas. Tom was full of rage but did not know how to act, so he climbed into the truck and got in the driver's seat. Then he took his hands off the wheel and screamed "No!" At that moment he threw his keys out the passenger door at Rick's chest and jumped out the driver's side of the vehicle. Tammy picked them up and climbed in the truck, saying, "Get in, Rick, we need to talk."

"Stay there, Tom, we will be right back; it is not as it seems," Rick slurred. Tom wondered how it got to this. Did he drive her to this with his lack of real love and understanding for so many years?

They knew Tom's scream would alert the

attention to the front of the house. Tammy started the engine and began to drive. Little Ronnie is outside, Tom thought, and instinctively began to sprint ahead of the truck. Tammy did not understand what he was doing and started to slow down, thinking he wanted to talk. But as she slowed, Tom kicked it in with a sprint up the hill. He did not understand how he thought that Ronnie was out, but he just knew it. He was only two houses away. Rick leaned out the passenger window and yelled, "What are you doing?" Tom's adrenalin helped push him ahead as Tammy drove slower. Through the dark he could barely see Ronnie at the top of the driveway, ready to take his last ride into the street. The sight confirmed his belief and gave Tom the added boost of adrenalin he needed.

Tom waved his hands and yelled "Stop, Tammy! Stop!"

Tammy knew what Tom was doing. He was going to get the kids. He was going to take her babies, so she put her foot down on the accelerator and sped the truck up. "No!" Tom screamed as he could see Ronnie start his descent. He had the truck beaten and knew he could get there in time. The truck came up on Tom as he pushed with all his might. He could only guess at the moment of impact and did not have the energy to try to stop Tammy. Ronnie was heading fast into the street. He leaped forward in front of the truck and pushed Little Ronnie back. Tammy slammed on the brakes, but not before the Suburban slammed into her husband.

Chapter 7

"I love my kids. I love Tammy. I love my kids. I love Tammy. I believe in God, the Father Almighty, Creator of Heaven and Earth." Tom kept repeating these words over and over again, hoping he would wake up.

"Wake up Thomas." Ollie broke through into his dream state. "You're home." Tom once more awoke to Ollie's presence. As before, the room was filled with a bright light. As he lifted his head and opened his eyes, he could begin to see images of people around him.

"Daddy!" his two girls screamed out in delight.

"Tammy," Tom spoke, looking up at his beautiful wife.

"Oh Tom," Tammy said, "we're so happy you're here with us."

Scotty just buried his head into Tom's chest. Ollie stood by watching all of it. Tom saw that all of his family knew Ollie was there with them. He turned and looked at Ollie confused.

"You're finally home, Tom."

"Everyone is dead?" Tom asked Ollie.

"Thomas, we are very happy with your last choice on earth. You gave your life for the safety of another. You are alive here. This is your heaven as you would want it. Your children are still your children." He looked up with tears in his eyes at his family.

He tried to understand the timeline or sequence of events. Did he die in prison? Did Scotty die first? Then he thought to himself, what does it matter? "I love all of you so much."

He felt absolutely wonderful. "Can it stay this way, Ollie?"

"Yes, it is God's will, Thomas. We will talk later so you will have an understanding, but the good news is that you made it. God loves you and this is a new and wonderful beginning for you and your family."

Tom put his arms around his family and began to cry and then laugh as they joined him. He stood up and began to walk. He was as strong as an athlete. "Daddy, come with us. We will show you around." With that, Tom walked off with his family down a path lined with beauty and wonder. "You made it,

Dad," Scotty said smiling. "We have been waiting for you."

"Oh son, I will never let you out of my sight again, God willing."

The End

Contact Chris Love
or order more copies of this book at

TATE PUBLISHING, LLC

127 East Trade Center Terrace
Mustang, Oklahoma 73064

(888) 361 - 9473

Tate Publishing, LLC

www.tatepublishing.com